What Mona Wants, Mona Gets

DYAN SHELDON

ILLUSTRATED BY
ELLA OKSTAD

First published 2005 by Walker Books Ltd
87 Vauxhall Walk, London SE11 5HJ

2 4 6 8 10 9 7 5 3 1

Text © 2005 Dyan Sheldon
Illustrations © 2005 Ella Okstad

The right of Dyan Sheldon and Ella Okstad to be identified as author
and illustrator respectively of this work has been asserted by them in
accordance with the Copyright, Designs and Patents Act 1988

This book has been typeset in Bembo Educational

Printed and bound in Great Britain by
Creative Print and Design (Wales), Ebbw Vale

British Library Cataloguing in Publication Data:
a catalogue record for this book
is available from the British Library

ISBN 1-84428-123-X

www.walkerbooks.co.uk

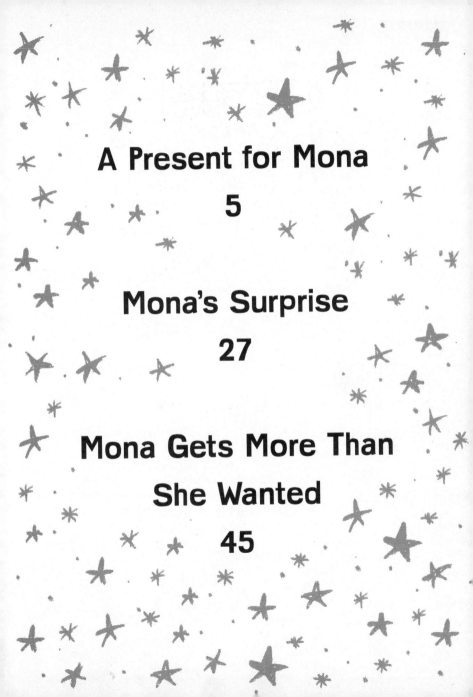

A Present for Mona

Mona and her mother were shopping
for a birthday gift for Mona's grandad.

Mona looked in the window of every
shop they passed. And in every window
she saw something she wanted.

A pair of
silver trainers.

A glittery
pencil case.

A neon
pink bag.

"Mona, please..."
begged her mother.
"What did I tell you?
We're shopping for your
grandad, not for you."

Mona scowled. "But I want —"

"Let's get away from here," said her mother. "Maybe we'll find a shop off the main road that has something perfect for Grandad."

Mona and her mother searched the
back streets without any luck.

"We seem to be going in circles," said
Mona's mother at last.

Mona pointed. "What if we go down there?"

Her mother frowned. "It looks like it's just an alleyway."

"There's a light," said Mona. "Maybe it's a café. I want chips and a drink."

But when they got there the light was
coming from a second-hand shop.

"I really wanted chips,"
moaned Mona.
Her mother
acted as if she
hadn't heard her.

"Well I suppose
we might as well
have a look,"
she decided.
Still whining
about chips,
Mona followed
her mother inside.

The shop was dark, and so packed with old things that it was hard to move.

Mona tugged on her mother's sleeve. "Let's go. We're not going to find anything in this dump."

"Mona, please!" Her mother nodded towards the counter. "Don't be rude."

It was then that Mona saw an old woman watching them from behind the counter with sharp, green eyes.

Mona's mother smiled at her. "I don't think I've ever seen a shop like this before."

"Of course not," snapped the old woman. "It's one of a kind."

Mona rolled her eyes. If you asked her, it was one too many.

Her mother explained what they were looking for.

The old woman nodded. "Well, there's something for everyone here."

"Not for me there isn't," muttered Mona.

The green eyes turned to her. "Well, perhaps if you look you'll find something you like."

Mona doubted that very much.

She followed her mother around the shop, grumbling.

"Mona, please… If you won't help, the least you can do is not hinder."

"But I want —" began Mona.

Suddenly the old woman was beside her, holding out a small wooden box.

"Here. Look at this till your mother's ready."

Mona scowled.

"Open it," ordered the old woman.

Mona did as she was told.

Inside the box was a crystal moon on a silver chain. One of Mona's friends had a necklace very like it. When you held it up to the light you could see a rainbow. Mona held up the necklace, but instead of a rainbow she saw trillions of stars.

They seemed so real that she felt as though she was falling through space.

"Mona!

Come on!"

Mona looked round, surprised to find her mother standing at the entrance with a parcel in her hands, ready to go.

"Oh, please," wailed Mona. "I really, *really* want this!"

"Well you can't have it. Now let's go."

"Please…" begged Mona. "I promise I'll never ask for anything again."

"Put it back," ordered her mother. "We have to go." But the necklace wouldn't leave Mona's hand. "Mona! What did I say? Put it back." Mona shook her fingers, but still the necklace didn't fall off.

"Take it."

Startled, Mona turned. She'd forgotten the old woman. "Pardon?"

"Take it," she repeated.

"Oh, thank you!" cried Mona. She did love getting presents.

"You'd better put it on, or you'll lose it." The old woman winked. "But be careful what you ask for in future, or you might just get it."

Mona happily fastened the necklace around her neck.

"Oh, don't worry," said Mona. "I'm never going to ask for anything else ever again."

Mona's Surprise

On Monday,
as she was getting
dressed, Mona
noticed the crystal moon in the
mirror. She stared at it for a few
seconds, wondering why she'd ever
wanted it in the first place. It was just
a dumb necklace. You couldn't even
see rainbows in it.

Mona went to toss
it in her jewellery box
with all the other necklaces
she never wore, but she
couldn't undo
the clasp.

She tried again

and again,

but it wasn't
any use.

Her mother couldn't get it off either.

Mona's mum pushed and pulled, but it wouldn't budge. "We don't have time for this now," she said. "We have to hurry, or we'll be late for your dentist's appointment."

Mona looked at a magazine while she waited for the dentist to call her. It was crammed with things she wished she could have.

"Oh, Mummy, look at those boots."

She held the magazine so her mother could see the picture.

"I want boots like those."

"Um…" said her mother.

On the next page it was a bright
yellow ski parka that caught Mona's
eye.

"Oh look, Mummy. I want that."
"Um…" said her mother.

PRINCESS

On the next
page it was
a pink party
dress.

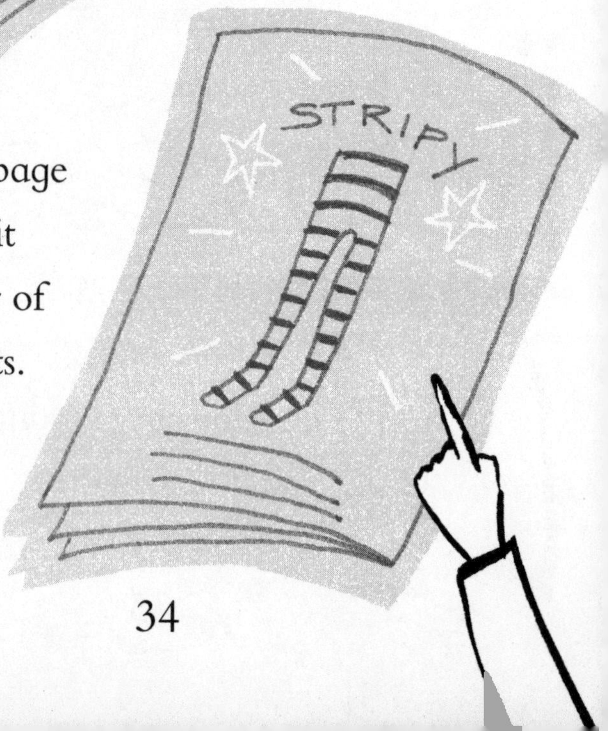

On the page
after that it
was a pair of
stripy tights.

STRIPY

34

"I thought you were never going to
want anything again as long as you got
that necklace," said Mona's mother.

Mona, of course, had completely
forgotten about her promise in the shop.

"I knew it wouldn't last,"
sighed her mum.

By the time she got home, Mona had already forgotten about the things she'd seen and wanted in the magazine ...

until she went to her room.

The pink party dress was hanging
from the door of the wardrobe.
Mona jumped in delight. Her mother
must have bought it to surprise her!

Then she saw the boots on the floor
beside the chest of drawers.
Mona's eyes moved around the room.
The ski parka was lying across the
foot of the bed.

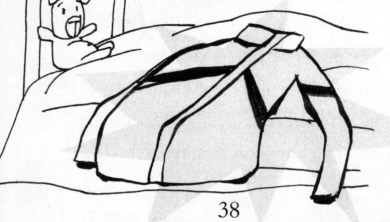

The tights were
neatly folded over the
back of her chair.

Shrieking
with joy, she
ran downstairs
to thank her mother.

Mona's mother looked round. "What are you on about? What things?"

"You know," said Mona, "the ones from the magazine."

Mona's mother had turned back to the TV. "What magazine?" she asked absent-mindedly.

Mona decided not to say any more.
She was afraid her mother might make
her give everything back.

Mona was distracted all through
supper, wondering how the new clothes
had found their way to her room.
If her mother hadn't given them to her,
who had?

It wasn't until she was getting ready
for bed that Mona remembered she was
still wearing the necklace.

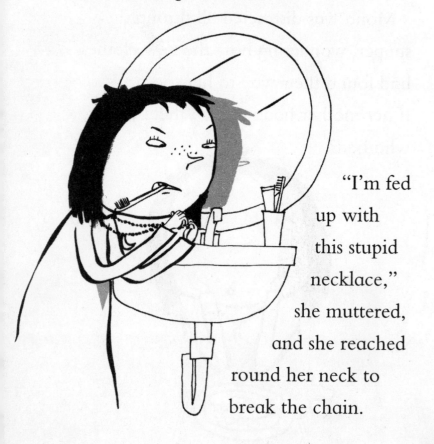

"I'm fed
up with
this stupid
necklace,"
she muttered,
and she reached
round her neck to
break the chain.

Which was when Mona heard the
voice of the old woman in the shop
once more.

*"But be
careful what
you ask for in
future, or you
might just get it…"*

Mona stared at herself in the mirror.

It was the necklace! She laughed out loud. That had to be it! The necklace would give her anything she wanted!

Mona danced around the bathroom. If she wasn't the luckiest girl in the world, she'd like to know who was.

Mona Gets More Than She Wanted

That night Mona dreamt about some of the thousands of things she'd always wanted and never got.

She dreamt about the pony and the swing set; the rabbits and the Wendy house; the tuba, the cowboy boots and the bicycle; ice-cream sundaes and burgers and chips.

"I want... I want...
I want..." Mona
mumbled over and
over in her sleep.
"I want... I want...
I want..."

It was such a good
dream that Mona
slept through her
alarm. She only woke
when her mother
started shouting,
"Mona! What are
you doing? Come
down and have your
breakfast!"

"Coming!" Mona shouted back.
As she opened her eyes, a rabbit
jumped over her.

I must still
be dreaming,
she thought.

She sat up –
and banged
her head on
a tuba.

Mona looked around.
The tuba wasn't the only
new thing in her room.

The swing set, the three-wheeled bicycle and the Wendy house were also new.

As were the rabbits.

The pony hadn't been there yesterday either.

Mona
touched the
necklace
she was
wearing
and laughed.
Of course. It had given her
what she wanted, even though she'd
wanted it when she was sound asleep!

"Mona!" her mother shouted again.
"Hurry up! It's a long drive to
Grandad's. I want to get going.
We don't want to be late for his
birthday party."

Mona managed to get out of
bed by climbing
onto her desk,

but she
couldn't even
see the carpet.

"Mona!" Her mother sounded angry.
"Hurry up!"

But Mona couldn't hurry up.

She had to
crawl under
the swing
set to get
to her
wardrobe.

And when
she reached
the wardrobe,
she discovered
that the rabbits
had been eating
her new pink
party dress.

"Mona!" Her mother sounded
very angry now. "If you're not
down here in **five minutes**,
I'll get someone to look after you
and I'll go on my own!"

"I'll be right there!"

Mona started searching frantically
through the new clothes heaped on the
floor, but there were too many to
choose from.

**"Four more
minutes!"**
shouted her
mother.

Mona took off
her pyjamas and
pulled on a red
tutu and a
sweatshirt that
said "Princess"
on the front.

"**Three!**" screamed her mother.

The pony
was standing
on her best shoes.

Mona yanked
her slippers from
under a giant
stuffed kangaroo
and put them on.

"**Two!**"

The Wendy house stood between Mona and the door.

"I want to get out… I want to get out…" chanted Mona in desperation.

Nothing happened.

"**Mona!**" Her mother was right outside the door, which she couldn't open because the Wendy house was in the way. "You let me in!"

"I'm coming!" Mona screamed back. But she wasn't going anywhere.

"That's it!" roared her mother. "Not only are you missing the party, but I'm not buying you anything new till next year."

"But I don't want anything!" wailed Mona. "I just want to go with you!" And she tugged on the necklace with such force that it broke and flew into the air.

60

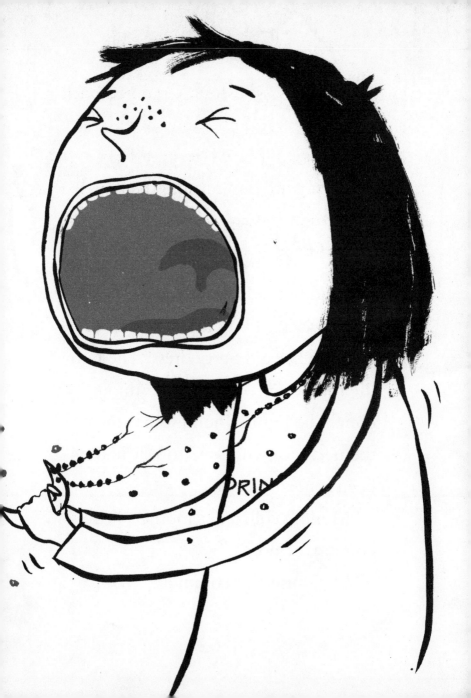

Mona rubbed her eyes.

She was standing in her bedroom wearing her old party dress. The pony, the rabbits and all the other things were gone. She put her hand to her throat: the necklace was gone too. It had all been a horrid dream.

"Mona!" called her mother. "Are you coming, or not?"

"Of course I'm coming!"

Mona stepped carefully over the rabbit poo that lay between her and the door.

Perhaps it hadn't been a dream after all.

Just in case, Mona was going to be very careful what she asked for in future.